A Father's Love

written by
KATRINA JOHNSON

illustrated by
ANGEL TRAZO

Published by Melanin Origins LLC

PO Box 122123; Arlington, TX 76012

All rights reserved, including the right of reproduction in whole

or in part in any form.

Copyright 2023

First Edition

The author asserts the moral right under the Copyright, Designs and Patents Act of 1988 to be identified as the author of this work.

This novel is a work of fiction. The names, characters and incidents portrayed in the work, other than those clearly in the public domain, are of the author's imagination and are not to be construed as real. Any resemblance to actual persons, living or dead, events or localities, is entirely coincidental.

All rights reserved. No part of this publication may be reproduced, stored in a retrieval system or transmitted, in any form by any means without the prior consent of the author, nor be otherwise circulated in any form of binding or cover other than that with which it is published and without a similar condition being imposed on the subsequent purchaser.

Library of Congress Control Number: 2022914703

ISBN: 978-1-0880-5764-3 hardback

ISBN: 978-1-0880-5196-2 paperback

To my loving son Landon, thank you for inspiring me in so many ways to write this book!

To my sweet daughter, Essence your constant encouragement means the world to me!

To my own father, Michael Johnson, Sr. "Daddy-O," I am forever grateful for your wisdom, love, and care. I love you!

To my loving family and friends, thank you for always cheering me on! Your support means more than you know.

To every young boy in the world, may you know that you are loved, you matter, what you do is important, and we are proud of you. Keep shining!

A boy needs a strong father to hold his hand and show him the way.

A boy needs a strong father to help him learn how to play and pray.

A boy needs a strong father to keep him safe from hurt and harm.

A boy needs a strong father so that he can learn and not alarm.

A boy needs a strong father to teach him how to grow from being a boy to being a man.

A boy needs a strong father to help him understand God's plan.

A boy needs a strong father to teach him how to love and forgive.

A boy needs a strong father to accept the responsibilities that help him live.

A boy needs a strong father to be in his life from the very beginning.

A boy needs a strong father
So that he can know that life is worth living.

A boy needs a strong father to help coach him, shape him, and mold him.

A boy needs a strong father to help him understand who he is and how much he matters in the world.

A boy needs a strong father
to teach him about love and respect.

A boy needs a strong father
Because, fathers, your voice matters above the rest.

A boy needs a strong father
To hold his hand and lead the way.

A boy needs a strong father
Because without you he will lose his way.

A boy needs a strong father to stand tall and strong.

A boy needs a strong father all the day long.

Answers to Four Key Questions That Sons Need to Know from Their Fathers

https://www.fatherhood.org/fatherhood/4-key-things-sons-need-from-their-fathers

1. Do I matter to you?
2. Do you love me?
3. Is what I do important to you?
4. Are you proud of me?

Positive Affirmation for Boys

I AM...
Brave
Kind
Strong
Full of goodness
Able to do amazing things

Positive Ways That Mentorship Impacts Children
https://www.casapacifica.org/news/blog/thepositiveeffectsofmentoring

- Healthier lifestyle choices
- Academic improvements
- An increase in self-confidence
- Improved behavior
- Better relationships with others

About the Author

Katrina Johnson

Katrina Johnson is a mother of two, award-winning professional school counselor, certified holistic life coach, registered trainer, and the award-winning author of *Penelope Embraces Her Uniqueness*. She holds a Bachelor's degree in Speech Communication, a Master's degree in Special Education, a second Master's degree in School Counseling, and a Principal's Certification. She is also skilled in Social Emotional Learning, Mindfulness, Self-Care and Stress Management.

As a school counselor and student support coordinator, she has worked with various organizations, student groups, parents, teachers, and administrators to help teach awareness about good character traits, positive social skills, and academic, career, social/emotional awareness, self-care and stress management.

She enjoys reading, journaling, genealogy research, listening to jazz music, time in nature, and spending quality time with her family and friends. She realizes that organizations, students, and their families face many challenges in today's world, and it is her daily pleasure to encourage, teach, coach, and guide them toward positive solutions and helpful resources to support their growth and needs.

Printed in the USA
CPSIA information can be obtained
at www.ICGtesting.com
LVHW012009170923
758353LV00003B/22